Poison Love

Bianca Holmes

Bianca Holmes

Copyright

Poison Love

Love is Blind. Soul Ties are Real.

Bianca Holmes

Bianca Holmes

Table of Contents

Bianca Holmes

POISON LOVE

Bianca Holmes

Chapter 1

"Here I am back to square one," I said as I lay in the bed. Ugh, I swear if it isn't one thing it's another. Sorry, you'll allow me to introduce myself. I am Porsha Evans. I am the CEO and Founder of "The Sisterhood". The sisterhood is basically a women group in a small town in LA where we come together and have "The Talk" about life, relationships, and goals. The goal of this group is to inspire and motivate all women, no matter the race. So far, the group has been progressing well, we are building every day. I am thankful to have this group because it keeps me going even on bad days. Speaking of such, my life is a living hell right now! My job, which I am one of the top lawyers, is stressful! Everybody wants to be innocent. Well newsflash, ya asses should have thought about that shit before ya got ya ass in trouble, and now I'm stuck trying to prove a case (rolls eyes)! On top of that is my husband with his aggravating sensitive ass! Lord, I swear if I wanted kids, I would have them. My husband's name is Chris. He stands about 6'2, brown eyes, low cut with deep waves, nice size body, pearly white teeth and he is packing! He is actually the head manager at the law firm I work at. Long story! I love that man to death, but I swear he drives me crazy. He gets a little full of himself until I knock him back to size and remind him, I am the prize! I am not conceited or anything, but I am confident and if he knows what I know, he'll stay on his shit. Other than that, he treats me like a queen. The sad thing is my schedule plus my group and his schedule; we barely have the time for each other. I hate it, but sometimes I enjoy that time being away. Overall, our marriage isn't perfect, Lord knows we have been through some rough patches, but that's another story we will get into. I guess I'll wrap this up, relax and get some rest! I got a big day ahead of me tomorrow and I'm going to need all the energy I can get! Goodnight!

Bianca Holmes

Chapter 2

(Yawns),

"Is it that time already!" I say, yawning

I swear I don't enjoy getting up, but when you are a go-getter, it is no time to sleep. As I'm getting out of bed, I see Chris is already gone. Nah I'm not going to jump the gun, but I'm not gon sit and act like I'm not getting fishy about things. I love my man true enough, but my trust is gone out of the window! Let me tell you why!

One day we came home from a long day of good laughs, and fun. Chris goes upstairs to run a bubble bath for us because I was ready to get it on. I had way too many drinks and I was ready to feel that ten-inch dick. Our night couldn't get any better, (well actually it was going too!) As I'm getting myself together, lusting, I hear a vibration from the counter; Of course, it was his phone, so I decided to see what the noise was about. It was a strange number texting.

Around our house we don't lock phones, neither do we check each other's phone, but it was something about my woman intuition telling me to go for it, and of course I went for it. I picked up the phone and I saw.

Hey baby, can't wait to see you tomorrow!"
I didn't even open the text; I read it from the screen. I said to myself, *"Oh so this nigga wants to creep."*It's all good. I'm not going to say shit to his ass, because two can play that game. When you play a woman like me, you better play those cards right. I'll play your deck and mine. He got me and the game twisted. I'm going to remain a lady though, no sweat because I'm going to still go and fuck and suck the shit out of him. My hormones are up too, I got a couple of nuts to bust.

He calls me upstairs to let me know he is ready for me to come up. I slowly take my clothes off and walk up the stairs butt naked. I entered our bedroom and he got the candles lit, the soft music playing, and the tub full of bubbles. My pussy is throbbing now; I'm ready to get fucked. He grabs me by the hand and guides me to the bed. He then begins to tongue kiss me as he slides his fingers in between my legs caressing my clit. Lord! I can feel myself about to buss, but I got to keep it together so I can buss on that dick.

As he began to feel my body jerk, he pulls his fingers out and starts penetrating my booty hole as he was sucking on my nipples. My man is a freak and I think that's why I may have ignored a lot of signs but bump all that the way he had my body feeling, I didn't even care.

I said, "Chris we got to make it to the tub before the water gets too cold."

He said, "Porsha fuck that water!" "This is my show, and it doesn't stop till' the well runs dry!"

I didn't have anything else to say, I let him have the control! He took those juicy lips and started sucking on my pussy! I bust within 2 mins all in his mouth.

"Damn girl", he said! Daddy pleasing the body!

I had to give him his props because Daddy did the damn thing.

"Yes Daddy", I said! I was about to get up to suck his dick, but he pushed me back down and told me to feel that pressure. He gave me just that. I got some long slow dick that night and we never did make it to the tub. Boy, was that a good night! Back to reality. That's how all the suspicions began. Let me jump in the shower and clean myself up. I got moist just thinking about how good he is! Ugh, I don't want to be here today, as I was saying pulling up at the courthouse! Who am I representing today (rolling eyes)? If it wasn't for the money I was making, I definitely wouldn't be here today! You can't depend on people nowadays, so you do what you got to do. As I'm walking through the doors, I saw a piece of dark chocolate I couldn't take my eyes off of. I had to keep my composure but Miss Pearly got to move. My hormones were already up from reminiscing. I sat in my seat ready to do what I got to do to get this case over with. "Where is Eugene," I said as I was getting impatient! Next thing you know all I smell is good ass cologne flying past my nose. I looked over to my right and it was Mr. Chocolate from the hallway. Damn! Why do I have to represent him? I felt my body getting all hot. I need to excuse myself, I yelled to the judge. "Take your time Mrs. Evans," he replied. I had to go to the bathroom to cool off. I don't know what it is about this man, but he got me wanting to know more about him! Get it together! I said to myself. You're married and you're representing him trying to keep him out the cells. What can he possibly do for me? I walked back to my seat ready to get started! Well, judging from the documentation I have, and from what you have, my client is innocent due to forgery. I have his ID right here and the signature does match. What you have looks like someone tried to trace it and failed your honor. The judge takes a look and says, "Well Mrs. Evans, you are right." That does indeed looks like a forgery. Mr. Eugene, you are free to go. Yessssss, I said in my head. That went by fast as hell. When you are on your job like you're supposed to be, that's what happens. As I'm approaching the door, I feel someone grab me by the hand. Well what do you know, it's Mr. Chocolate. I suddenly begin to get weak (don't judge me y'all)! Thank you, Mrs. Evans, that really meant a lot to me. I never had a woman to hold me down, even though it's your job! I wanted to jump in his arms right then. You're welcome Mr. Eugene; I do what I got to do to make sure my clients stay out of trouble. Well, I'm going to need your number, he said. No, you not! I said with aggression! He said, "you do know I have to check in with you right?" Oh yeah, that is right, I said as I calmed down. The last thing I needed was him thinking I wanted him; I was already lusting for him. I gave him my card and we went our separate ways. I pulled up to my organization club to check on my ladies to see how everything is going. It was going how I thought it would be, great! I can go home and relax now. I made it to my house, kicked off my shoes, turned on some Dru Hill, poured a glass of wine, slipped into my nightclothes, and sat in front of the fireplace. I swear it felt good to have the house alone. My husband should be here soon, so let me enjoy the time I do have. I can tell our marriage is going downhill because nothing is the same anymore.

There's barely any conversation, but the sex is still there most of the time. I started to think about Eugene. That smile and his smell had me. I began to feel tipsy, so I picked up my phone scrolling back and forth through it debating if I wanted to "check" on him. I knew it was wrong and against my job, but it felt so right. I started to question myself. Is it worth it? Is it worth my job? I had more than enough money behind me if I was to take that route, but why do I want to chance it on someone

I'm representing? It's way past hours, and Chris still hasn't made it here yet. I call his phone and it goes straight to voicemail. Okay, I see where this is going. There is no need for me to get upset, it is what it is. I starred at Eugene's number for a good five minutes before I sent him a text. Yes, I sent him a text! I tried to unsend it, but it was too late. Now here I am pacing back and forth trying to figure out what the hell I just did. Ughhhhhhhh! *Bing* my cell phone goes off and now my heart is racing. I opened up the text and read it (*what's up beautiful*). This is wrong on so many levels but bump it. I'm feeling good; my husband isn't home, why not. (*What are you doing right now?*) I replied. (*Nun much how about you?*) he said. There goes that thuggish talk. I don't know if you'll know it or not but isn't nothing like a hood nigga. Imma just be real. You know what they say about them (chuckles). (*nothing really but sipping on this wine while I'm listening to Dru Hill*) I said. (*sounds like you are feeling good over there, I wish I was over there with you*) he said. That's when all the trouble came. (you could be, but I'm married, I could come to you) "oh, shit did I just say that! (come on over) he said, sending the address. What am I getting myself into? Should I go or should I stay? Hmmmm! *Bing* My phone goes off again but it's Chris this time. I opened the message: (Hey baby, I'm staying out with the fellas tonight I'm going to stay with Shawn tonight. Bullshit! I know he is lying, I am not mad though because now I can do my thing. I slipped my panties off, put on my slippers and headed out the door. I made it to his house and there he was standing at the door with some Hanes briefs on and all I could smell from the doorway was that good ass cologne. I didn't even make it in the house good. He threw me up against that wall and started kissing and caressing my body. Oh shit, this is really happening.

Chapter 3

Man! What in the hell have I done? I have sparked up a new flame, but I swear it felt so right! One thing I do know is that I or my husband didn't make it home last night and if I could replay every-thing that happened with Eugene, I would do it all over again! Here I am thinking Chris was a freak; He ain't got anything on Mr. Chocolate! I rolled over to see that he was gone. "Where the hell is he," I said to myself. Next thing I know, I heard my name being yelled from inside the kitchen. "Mrs. Evans, I made you some breakfast." I thought to

myself I haven't had that in a while, my man does-
n't even do that for me. "Coming," I said. Boy, did
he have that kitchen smelling good and he cooked
butt naked. Lord why? I said to myself. I felt Miss
Pearl throbbing again. Eugene I got to go! I am not
even supposed to be here right now, this is so
wrong! He took me by the hand, looked me in the
eyes, and said, "Your secret is safe with me, we are
both grown." I felt a little relieved, but it still wasn't
right. I know my husband is out doing his thing,
but two wrongs don't make a right and I should
have known better to let a Lil wine get me over
here. I got up to go get my things and all I could feel
was his hard manhood against me while he is whis-
pering in my ear telling me he's sorry. I turned
around, we caught eye contact and it went from
there. All I know is we ended up in the shower! He
caressed my clit with his tongue so much; I know I
had about 5 orgasms. He rocked my world and I felt
like I was falling deep for him. A little too deep. I
didn't want to feel this way but let's be real I am getting no love back at home. I finally managed to put
my clothes on and headed to my house. As I'm
pulling up in the driveway, I saw Chris, car in the
driveway. "Oh Shit," I'm saying to myself. What am
I going to tell him? I don't know but it better be
quick because here he comes. "Hey, Sweetie," you

ok? He said. "Chris you got some damn nerve to even be asking me anything when yo ass ain't even come home last night!" "Ah Porsha I did come home last night, you didn't!" he said with anger. I'm thinking to myself like think Porsha think. How the hell I'm going to get myself out of this one? "I know I didn't come home last night!" I said with rage. (A way to flip the script). "I stayed at Jasmine's house!" Jasmine is a homegirl. Nothing more, nothing less. We hang out sometimes, but I don't trust her as far as I can throw her. "I went to her house because you pissed me off saying that you were staying out with the guys which I know you were lying. I know you were with a bitch Chris!" "Babe," he said with a calm voice while he was pulling out his phone. Here are the pictures right here I and the guys were at the bar getting toasted. I wouldn't lie to you Porsha, you're my wife. As bad as I wanted to fall for the bullshit, I wasn't! Maybe he was out with the fellas, but he still was fucking around. I finally got out of the car and as I was entering the front door, I smell food. I questioned Chris about the smell and to my surprise he made me breakfast. Oh, hell no, this cannot be happening. I ate it, but all I could think about was Eugene. I didn't get to eat his breakfast, but he gave me something better! I got hot just thinking of his name. Chris approaches me, picks a fork up, and started feeding me. I wasn't in the mood, but I took it for what it was because he is my husband at the end of the day! I quickly ate, got dressed, kissed Chris and headed out to go chill with the ladies today at the clubhouse. They were so happy to see me when I got there, the vibes were amazing. I love these ladies because anytime I need a shoulder to lean on, they are always there. "Okay ladies, what's been going on today?" Everything is going great; I was thinking we could do a community cookout. "I think that would be a great idea," I said. When I get home, I'll put everything into motion, you ladies take a break you have done enough. "Thanks Porsha," Shelia said

Chapter 4

Ok Ladies! Here is everything that is needed for the cookout, if you need anything else, let me know before my husband gets here. Chris is on the way to cook on the grill; he sure can throw down. Today is going to be a great day, I said to myself. The weather is right, my spirits are in a good place right now; I'm not letting anyone come in between that! It smells like heaven in here, my husband said as he kissed me on the cheek. You ladies are doing an excellent job, reminds me of my mom's cooking, he said.

Thank you honey, I replied him. The joy I feel right now is indescribable. I'm about to turn on some music and pump this cookout up. (Bing) my cell phone goes off. I go to pick it up and guess who it is? Yea you are right, it's Eugene. Here goes the devil! He sure knows how to show up on a good day, but no worries! I placed the phone back down. I feel bad I took it that far with him, but I can't take it back. The only thing I can do at this point is to ignore it and hope it goes away. Although I did enjoy him don't get me wrong, I'm a whole married woman. Lord, if I could take it back I would. Baby, are you okay? Chris said as he walked up to me. Yes, babe I am, I said with a fake smile on my face. Ok just making sure, he said. Hey baby, he said. I invited one of my boys I grew up with. Ok, that's fine I said. Everyone is welcome. I started to think about Jasmine. I know I don't talk to her as much, but she still is a cool person. She has got me out some shit, but that's another story. I dialed her to see what she was up to. She wasn't doing anything but sitting around the house, so I invited her to the cookout. I told her about Chris' homeboy that was coming, so she told me to give her a few minutes and she will be down. I'm sitting here like look at me trying to play matchmaker. Jasmine stands about 5'3 145 pounds. She has wavy hair and is very outspoken. She is very beautiful. I give credit when it's due. A lot of women of our color are so quick to put the next woman down. For What! We as sisters have to come together and uplift each other as well as inspire one another. (Bing) I got another text. What does this nigga want? I looked at my phone and to my surprise, it's Chris telling me to come out and meet his friend because he is trying to burn the food. Ladies I'm about to step outside for a minute and I'll be right back, I said as I was walking out. I swear, as soon as I got to the last step, my jaw dropped. It was Eugene. What in the hell, I said to myself? I didn't know what to do at this point. I couldn't run because then it'll look suspicious, so I had no choice but to walk over. Hey fellas, I said trying to keep myself together. Eugene turned around and his facial expression said it all. Good thing my husband wasn't looking because it would've been some shit. I'm Porsha, I said as I stuck my hand out to shake his hand. I'm Eugene he said as he stuck his hand out. I could pass out right now, but I got to keep it together. My husband got the lid down on and started telling me their lifestyle stories. I didn't want to hear that shit, I just wanted to take my ass home. My good day turned quick, but we did play it off well. Porshaaaaaa, I heard from behind me. It was Jasmine. I hugged her so tight; I was saved by the bell. How u doing girl, I said. I'm doing good, she said. I was trying to get here as soon as I can, but the traffic is hell. What's up Jasmine, Chris said as he was flipping the burgers. Hey Chris, she replied. Let me not be rude, I said to myself. Jasmine this is Chris' friend Eugene, and Eugene this is my friend Jasmine. Nice to meet you they both said. Jasmine pulled me to the side and whispered, "Dang he fine!" You need to hook a sister up! As bad as I wanted to say something to her about what happened, I didn't. Jasmine has a mouth on her. She may not mean any harm by it, but she gossips and tells everything. I got you, I said. I'll mention something to Chris. Ok, she said! I'm about to go back in and prepare the tables so everybody can eat. I'll come and help, Jasmine said. Hey Miss Jasmine, Eugene yelled out! Save me a seat next to you. Ok! Jasmine replied. In my head, I had some things I want to say to him, but I can't. I should be happy though because this could be my break away from him. Ok everyone come on in, I yelled! The smile on everyone's face took my mind off everything. Positive vibes filled that room, and I was happy. This is what my organization is all about. I cleaned up the place after everyone left and invited jasmine to go out and have a drink. I just wanted to be nosey to see what she and Eugene were talking about. I don't need any problems. We got to Sky City the new bar they had just opened in downtown and had 3 shots. It was live in there, but I liked the atmosphere. So, I said to Jasmine as we began to talk. How did things go with you and Eugene? A big smile came across her face. It was like a kid in a candy store. I think I'm in lust, she said. I burst out laughing, almost spitting my drink out. Are you serious? I said. Yes! She said. His voice alone got me wanting to see what he is about. I can tell he is hood, and you know what they say about hood niggas. Oh, don't I know, I said in my head. He invited me over, she said. I might just take him up on that offer. Whatever floats your boat, I said to her. You only live once (yolo)! You are absolutely right Porsha, she said. She then picks up her phone and lets him know that she is coming over. I then began to reminisce on the things we did and how good he felt. Damn why I have to give that up, I said to myself. I'm feeling good as hell right now, I want him. I picked up my phone and contemplated if I was going to hit him up or not. I called Chris to see what he was up to. He answered and said he wasn't feeling good and that he was about to go to bed. I told him that I was going to stay over at Jasmine's house since she stayed closer to where we were ok. He was ok with that and hung up the phone. I asked jasmine if she was ready to go. She replied yea and to take her to Eugene house and she'll pick up her car tomorrow. I replied ok as she started to give me directions as if I ain't already know, but I played along. We pulled up and Jasmine got out of the car. I shut my car off and decided to walk to the door with her. She's feeling good so she really ain't paying attention. Eugene opens the door with a smirk on his face. I played it off like I had to use the bathroom. He tells Jasmine to make herself at home while he shows me where the upstairs bathroom is. As soon as we make it upstairs, I threw him against the wall and started to kiss him. He sticks his hand under my dress and started to rub and finger my pussy. I wanted to scream at how good it felt but Jasmine was downstairs. I moved and told him to go back down to check on her. He came back up and said she was passed out on the couch. Why did he say that? I ripped his shirt off, pulled his pants down, and started to suck his dick. I don't know why, but it tasted good, or it could've just been the alcohol. He started to moan. I was going to rock his world tonight. I got up, pushed him on the bed, and started riding his dick. He started grabbing my nipples, which boosted my hormones up and made me ride him even harder. My moan started to get even louder, I had to catch myself. It was good I started not to even care. He grabbed me by the waist and held me real tight, telling me he was about to cum. I stayed on top and told me to cum so I can feel that dick jerk. Next thing I know he let out a loud noise and burst. What the hell! Jasmine said as the door flung open. Damn it Eugene! I was speechless. I don't even know what to say. Jasmine just stared at me as I got up. As I walked past her, she grabbed me by the arm. I looked at her like bitch get off me. I was already caught anyway, thanks to dumbass; it couldn't get any worse than that. I looked and told her I was sorry and that it just happened. She looked at me, laughed, and said girl you good. We homegirls, I knew you wanted him as bad as I did. Look at him, who can resist that. I then said, you're right but it shouldn't have happened. Eugene then gets up and said ladies; we can always make this a 3sum. I slapped him and said no, I don't get down like that. The next thing I know, Jasmine starts rubbing on my clit. I slapped her hand, saying what the hell Jas, even though it did feel good. I can't get jiggy with this type of shit. She then replied we are all here, why not. Eugene then begins to hug me from behind as he started rubbing my nipples. Jasmine then gets on her knees and started sucking on my pussy. As bad as I wanted to kick her ass, I couldn't.

It felt so damn good, I just let it happened. I can feel his dick getting hard again as I was moaning. He then bends me over and started hitting it from the back. I moaned aloud as hell because it felt so good. Jasmine then starts kissing him. He begins to pound harder. He then told me to lie on the bed. As I lay on the bed, Jas started eating my pussy again and he began stroking her from the back. I could not believe I was doing this shit. This was way beyond me, but I guess there is a first time for everything. "Lord, why must the wrong things feel so right?" I said to myself. The more it happened the more I enjoyed it! That was good, Jasmine said. "Hell yea," Eugene said! I'm about to go home and shower, Jasmine said. I'm coming with you, I responded. I already told Chris I was staying over at your house. Ok, that's cool Jasmine said. Eugene sat down with a smirk on his face. He obviously is no friend of Chris, but I was no better than he is. Well, we will see you later, I yelled to Eugene as we were walking out of the house. True, he yelled back! As we got in the car, we burst out laughing. This was some crazy shit, but yolo as they say it. As soon as I got to Jasmine's house I passed out. Today was very long and unexpected; I know I'm taking tomorrow off. Goodnight!

POISON LOVE

Bianca Holmes

Chapter 5

Girl, get up, Jasmine said as she was shaking me. What! I said with attitude. We just went to bed, why the hell is she waking me up? "Girl get up, Chris is out there and he looks pissed!" she said. I jumped up like it was somebody coming after us. "Oh shit!" What the hell is he doing here? I got up to go outside to see what was up. "What the fuck Porsha, Chris screamed!" I'm sitting here like what the hell. I'm lost right now. "After all the shit we have been through, you go do some fucked up shit, he said. At this point, I'm lost. What are you talking about

Chris? I said. Oh, don't act like you don't know! I know you have been fucking Eugene! He yelled. I looked like I saw a damn ghost. I don't know what to do at this point. I swear my heart stopped beating; I was just waiting on God to take me home. I looked back at Jasmine. "I always knew you were a trifling bitch, but you really gon scoot this low?" What the fuck Porsha, she replied in anger. I had nothing to do with this shit; I'm just as shocked as you! At this point, I didn't trust her ass because how the hell else Chris gon know, he is no damn psychic. Jasmine ain't tell me shit! Chris yelled. Both of you'll need to be ashamed of yourselves. Jasmine then yells at him, "What the fuck are you talking about, don't bring me in your shit!" Chris then yells, "Oh bitch, you deserve the blame as well because you were fucking Eugene as well!" Jasmine then looks speechless. Damn, we are both caught. How do you know Chris, I said? I had to break the silence. I mean we were already caught. "Eugene sent me the video, he said." I said to myself, "No this nigga didn't!" I knew I shouldn't have even gotten myself involved with this nigga. I dialed his number so fast; I forget my husband was standing in front of me! "Eugene that was some lame shit you pulled!" I said. You really sent my husband a video of us tonight. You a bitch-made nigga! In a calm voice, he said, "Send me the address I'll explain everything. I hung up the phone and sent the address. We gon get down to the bottom of this shit. About 10 minutes later Eugene pulls up. As soon as he got out of the car I wanted to slap the taste out his mouth. Chris daps him up and says, "Thanks for looking out man!" Eugene with that slick ass smirk on his face says, No Problem! It took all of me not to knock that punk ass nigga out. I felt that hood girl coming back up outta me. "That was some lame shit Eugene, Jas said. I have my reasons, he replied." Well what the fuck was the reason, I yelled!" It was payback! Payback, I screamed! Payback for what? Eugene starts to explain; well, your husband, a good friend of mine, is fucking my babymama! Before I knew it, I punched the hell out of Chris. I needed to release that. What the hell he is talking about Chris, I yelled. I don't know, Chris replied. What are you talking about man, Chris asked Eugene? Man, you have been fucking my babymama Ashley! I know because I have seen you two together and when I confronted her, she owned up to it. Chris sat there with a stupid look on his face. As bad as I wanted to jump on his ass, I didn't. I was enjoying this shit because I already knew he was cheating anyway. Chris began to stumble over his words, I'm sorry man. I got to admit I was messing with her, but I never knew she was your babymama man. You know me and you know we go way back; I would never do any shit like that. Eugene began to laugh out loud. It's all good bro; I just hit your wife. I want you to feel what I felt. I knew she was cheating but I never knew with who until one day I decided to follow her and saw her jump in her car with you. It crushed me, so I knew I had to return the favor. I didn't know man, Chris said. I understand that but the principle of it all is that this has been going on for some time now, Eugene replied. So, Chris, I said. You sit here and confront me on some shit, meanwhile yo ass out here cheating and which I already knew you were, just didn't know with who. I'm sorry baby, Chris replied. Oh no you ain't sorry, you are only sorry because you got caught, I said. Hold up now Porsha, he said. Let's not forget your ass out here not only cheating but having 3sums, something you always cursed me out about when I asked! Well, Chris it just happened! We weren't intimate like we were anymore and when I met Eugene I just went for it. So, you know Eugene, Jas butted in. Yes, I said. I met him at the courthouse when I had to represent him. I kind of figured that she said. The way you both caught eye contact when I walked in made me now something was up. I was torn up, but not that damn tore up. So how long has this been going on, Chris asked? Does it matter? I asked. You know what, I have had enough of this, I said. This is too much for one night. Jas I will call you; Eugene I have nothing to say to you at this point, and Chris, we will finish this up when we get home. Jas shut the door and turned the porch light off, Eugene hopped in his car, and we left.

Bianca Holmes

Chapter 6

I woke up with a damn migraine. To my surprise, Chris had some meds and orange juice waiting by the bedside. O I am done with his ass yet! We didn't get to talk last night, because I didn't have the energy. As soon as we arrived at the house I passed out. Rise and shine, Chris said as he was coming through the door. Good morning, I said with a slight attitude. I wanted to curse him out again, but what we both did was wrong. About last night, he said. I apologize. I should not have been stepping outside our marriage. The temptation was there, and I fell for it! I do not love her Porsha! Ugh! I said to myself. I guess I got to put my pride to the side and apologize as well. I apologize to you as well Chris, I replied. I let my hormones get the best of me and fell vulnerable. I was not thinking Chris and I'm sorry. He came over, looked me in my eyes deeply and told me he loved me. I swear I felt that through my soul. We both messed up, so we can't put the blame on each other and the bible says until death do us part. I kissed him slowly and told him I loved him. Why did I do that? His manhood stood straight up. I started to caress it slowly. I know I did what I did last night, but this is my husband. I can tell you'll one thing, that makeup sex was the best. My husband fucked me so good it had me in my feelings a little bit. You know that dick good when it gets you emotional and to know that there's another woman who had it. That's what kills me. After we finished, he told me to get washed up and put on my best fit because he had something planned for us. A big smile came across my face. I'm loving today already. As I got in the shower, I couldn't help but think how Eugene was doing. Even though I didn't like the way he went about doing things, I still had some part in it. I felt like I had feelings for him, but enough of that, I am about to have a great day out with my husband. I got out of the shower, dried off, and grabbed the lotion. My phone began to ring. I got scared for a moment because I don't need any extra problems. I looked and it was Jas ass. *(Hello)* I said. *(Heyygirllll)* Porsha replied sounding all excited. *(Nothing much girl getting dressed about to head out)* I Said. *(*Where are *you going?)* She asked. *(Chy out with Chris, I guess with all that happened last night he planned something girl. He just told me to get dressed, what are you up to?)* I asked. *(That is what'sup, that's sweet of him)* she said! *(and nothing much girl I got to tell you some news).* *(what'sup)* I said. Well after you all left, Eugene hit me up. I cursed him out at first, but we talked and put it behind us. Anyways girl he is going out of town to the Bahamas and he invited me to go, and you know I couldn't turn that down I need a getaway. (O snap, get it girl) In my fake voice. I don't know why but I got in my feelings. I knew it wasn't anything serious between me and Eugene, but I was feeling him a lot. I got to get it together. *(Yes girl)* Jas replied. *(Let me get myself together, Eugene will be here soon.)* *(Okay girl ttyl)* I said. I reached into my closet to get my sexy red knitted maxi dress to put on. I was waiting for the right time to put this on. The weather is feeling right and today is going to be special. I did my make-up, did my hair, and headed downstairs.

Damn baby you look gorgeous, Chris said with a surprised look on his face. Well-baby you told me to get dressed up and I did exactly that, I said. We left the house and went to the gas station to fuel up before we get to our destination. As we pulled up, guess who the hell we saw, Eugene. Boy, the devil sure does know when to show up, I said to myself as I was rolling my eyes. Chris gets out to pump gas, then I saw him walk over to Eugene. Oh Shit! I rolled the window down to listen. I couldn't really hear anything, but from what I could hear they were apologizing to each other. One thing I can say about guys is that they can brush shit off, but us females, hell no! Hell would have to freeze over first! I knew I was looking good, so I decided to get out of the car and get some gum from the store. I swear, Eugene's mouth dropped, but Chris didn't catch that. I'll be back babe, I yelled to Chris. I could feel them watching me from behind along with everyone else and I loved it. As I and Chris headed down the road, we talked a little. He didn't say too much, but he did say they talked about what had happened and vowed never to do that again as homeboys. I agreed, but how do I hide these feelings I have for his friend as well? I do not know, and I don't even want to think about it. I felt another migraine coming. "Close your eyes baby,

Chris said." I closed my eyes and as we got closer to where he was taking me, I heard music. Okay, you can open now, he said. Oh my gosh! I said as tears filled my eyes. He brought me to the place on the beach where he proposed to me at! There were candles lit, musicians, my favorite wine, and my favorite food. I began to cry. It felt like the first time, all those memories started rushing back to me. I ran up, hugged my husband, and thanked him. He whispered, after all, we have been through, and all that I have done to hurt you, you deserve the world baby. I started crying even harder. I should not have stepped out on my husband because now I feel like I'm caught up in a love triangle. "I have one more surprise baby, but it can wait till after we have eaten, Chris said. Lord, my evening could not get any better than this. I got to give my husband his props. He was slacking, but this makes up for it and I am appreciating it all. As time goes by with nothing but smiles and laughs, I decided to get on my Facebook page to post these moments in a group called "The Marriage Club." As I started scrolling down my timeline, I came across Jas page. She went live a few hours ago so I decided to watch it to see what was up with her and Eugene at the Bahamas. Look at me being nosey. I pressed play and they looked like they were having the time of their life.

They actually look like they were in love, and from what she was showing, he looked like he was waiting on her hand and foot. From massages to rose petals and bubble baths, etc. I was slick jealous because I had feelings for him but there was nothing I could have done at this point. I put the phone down and continued my special day with Chris. "Ok baby, Chris said." I told you I had a surprise for you so close your eyes. In my mind, I was saying, "I'm tired of closing my eyes" (giggling). Open up Porsha, he said. You'll my husband outdid himself. He upgraded my wedding ring, and it was the most beautiful ring I have ever seen. Here come the tears. I am a big water bag. I could not thank him enough and I was ready to show this off. Chris grabbed me tight and said, "Baby I'm sorry and I don't want to lose you. I will walk to the end of the world if that means having you in my life forever." I began to think to myself like; do I really want to give all of this up for someone who really has nothing to offer but some dick. I mean what else can Eugene really do for me, I helped get him out of trouble. No marriage is perfect, and my husband is definitely worth keeping our marriage together. Thank you for everything, I said to Chris. I'm sorry for what I have done as well, and I promise it will never happen again. "Just let it go, he replied." We are on to better things now. The wind started picking up and I asked Chris if he was ready to go. His response was, "We are staying here tonight babe, I got us a tent over by the ocean so we can listen to the sound of the waves while we're making love tonight." That was one of my fantasies, so I loved the sound of that, that was like music to my ears. Chris had the tent set up with candles and my favorite chocolates with some Rkelly playing. I was going to rock his world in this tent tonight and hope that it didn't fall over. I unzipped his pants and started slowly stroking his dick with my mouth. I was gon make this all about him tonight. I wasn't even five minutes in, and he was about to cum. Either he had been holding back or I was just sucking it good as hell. I was gon turn it up a notch, so instead of him nutting in my mouth, I let him shoot all over my face. It was shocking to him because he knows I don't play shit like that especially when my hair is done, but fuck it imma be his playground tonight. Once he was done, he thought that was it. I got it back up again and started riding the tip of his dick from the back. He moaned so loud I know the fish at the deep end of the ocean heard his ass. I loved it though, I wanted to make my man feel good. Before I knew it, he busted without warning. I felt every last bit of that. All I heard him say when he thought we were done was,

"Damn girl." "Chris get your ass up, I yelled!" One more round. "Porsha, I don't think I can go another round, he said." I ignored what he said and got it right back up. I rocked his world that whole night, then kissed him goodnight. I went to bed with sweet dreams.

Chapter 7

Months went by and I have not seen nor heard from Jas or Eugene but judging from Facebook and Instagram, they were dating and in love. I was actually happy for them both. My life was starting to come together. I and my husband made more time for each other and we had sex on a daily basis. My organization was going great as usual, we were still recruiting young and older women daily and my job started to smooth out, so it was less stressful. I thanked God every day for this. I was starting to get sick a lot, but I thought nothing of it at first. One day I decided to go to the hospital to see what was going on because I was told there was a virus going around. Once I got there and waited on my results, I got the news that I didn't want to hear. I was PREGNANT! My heart started racing and I started to feel really nauseated. I had to calm down. I wasn't ready for kids! What am I going to do? I left and made an appointment with my OBGYN the next day. As the time got close, I was starting to feel more and more nervous. I was hoping it was a mistake. I got to the back to get a sonogram and not only was I pregnant I was already three months. I wondered where my extra weight came from, I thought it was because I and Chris were going out to eat regularly. My heart started to race again because I was messing around with Eugene around that time. I ain't know what I was to do or how I was to explain this to Chris. Not only was I cheating, I was also being careless with it. I would say this day couldn't get any worse, but I won't because every time I do say it won't, it always does! I got back home and starting to pace back and forth to see how I was going to handle this shit. I definitely wasn't trying to reach out to Eugene. Think Porsha Think! (Knock Knock). I hear a loud bang on the door. I calmed down, got myself together, and answered it. When I opened the door, there stood a light-skinned woman with a newborn baby. She looked no older than 30. "Can I help you?" I said to the woman. "Is Chris here?" she replied. "No, he's not, I'm his wife!" "What can I help you with?" I said to her again. " I'm not here to cause any trouble, but I'm Ashley." she said. "I and Chris have been seeing each other for a while and from what he told me he was single. I knew I shouldn't have believed his lying ass!" At this point, I invited the bitch in because I wanted to hear this shit. My mind was instantly off my problems. We began to talk, and she basically told me how Chris was out playing family with her and her kids up until she got pregnant with his baby. She said once she told him that he left her high and dry, that was when she did some research and found out where he lived. She kept apologizing to me and I couldn't be mad even though I did want to make grab the bitch by her hair, but for what? It won't solve a thing. It then dawned on me that this was Eugene's babymama and now she may possibly have a baby by my husband. I did take a look at the baby and the baby did have features of him. I began to feel sick and ran to the bathroom to throw up. She followed me to the bathroom and asked me if I was ok. I told her I was okay and explained to her that I was pregnant as well and that Chris doesn't know. I didn't explain to her that it could possibly be her babydaddy's. This is some shit right here! Just when my life was coming together, it took a turn for the worst. I won't lie, I was mad and upset as hell. I couldn't even think straight. She was about to leave, but I convinced her to stay because Chris had some explaining to do. I'm not going to lie; the baby was gorgeous as hell. Kind of had me ready to have mine. Time went by and we talked. I know it may be weird being that she is the "other woman", but I didn't have the energy to react the way I wanted to especially with this precious baby here. I can't make any promises on how this is going to end when he gets home. "Baby I am home," Chris said as he came through the door singing. This nigga got some nerve, but he is definitely about to be in for a big surprise. "Hey Honey," I said with a fake smile. A package came for you in the living room. A bigger smile came across his face and he said, "ok, must be the tools I ordered off Amazon." It's tools alright, I said with a smirk across my face! The baby started to whine, and Chris runs off into the living room to see where the noise was coming from. His face went from sweet to sour, then that's when all the commotion began. "Ashley, what the hell are you doing at my house?" Chris said yelling! "Now the question is why you left when I told you I was pregnant, and why didn't you tell me you had a wife bastard!" I wanted to butt in and say some things, but I let them have it. I will talk when the timing is right. "Ashley, I don't even know if that baby is when you were hoeing around then and was acting like I was the only one!" Chris replied. (Whether I was hoeing or not and which I wasn't nigga you weren't even being real. I let you be around my kids, even pick them up from after school, and you never had the nerve to tell me you were married! That's fucked up!" Chris had the hush mouth because he knew he had fucked up, especially with denying me. Ashley then screamed, "We can get a DNA test but best believe when the results come out, you ass will be going on child support!" "Porsha I'm sorry all these happened, and I had no intentions of hurting you, but your husband is a lying son of a bitch and need to help take care of what he created!" I looked at Chris with tears in my eyes and slapped the piss out of him. I hit him so hard he stumbled backward and fell towards the wall. His nose started to bleed nonstop. You think I got his ass some tissue? Hell No! He deserved all of that and some more! I was so fired up it was get-back time. I know two wrongs don't make a right, but he will feel what I feel. "Well since everybody bringing shit out, I'm ready to speak!" I screamed. "Chris I can't believe this shit;

how could you do some shit like this to me?" You deny me then play family man to another bitch and her kids? That shit hurts! I felt rage all over me then, that's when I knew it was time for revenge! "Since I have been in the dark about everything, let me shed a little light!" "Chris! You know you hurt me to the core right, but I got something to tell you." Chris looked at me like he was anxious to see what was to be said. I can't wait to see his facial expression. "I'm pregnant, I said." He then looked at me with tears in his eyes and apologized. "No need to do that just yet, because that ain't all, I said in my evil voice." Chris and Ashley stared at me in fear! "I think I need to leave, Ashley said." This is way too much for me. "No don't go, I replied." I think you need to hear this! Ashley sat back down and took a sip of her drink. All hell was finally broken loose. "Not only am I pregnant, but I'm also three months pregnant, and the baby may not be yours. Chris jumped up so fast, I swear it was like lightning flashing before my eyes. He put his hands around my neck and choked the fuck out of me. Good thing Ashley was there because otherwise, I would've been dead! I could've called the police, but I didn't. Instead, I let out a loud laugh and said, "How you gon get mad?" "The shoe doesn't feel good on the other foot now does it?" He looked like he wanted to kill me, but he replied, "Fuck you bitch!" I laughed again. Ashley sat there looking confused on why she had to be there. So I broke her the news. " O yea, your babydaddy Eugene may be the father!" I said. She sat there in disbelief. "Oh, you are the bitch he was dodging me for?" I said with a smirk, "I guess I am!" Surprisingly, she did not come at me, because I was ready to let that bitch have it. Things all of a sudden got quiet. Ashley then picked up her phone and dialed a number. "Eugene you mother fucker!" She screamed at him. I can hear Jas in his background asking who the hell that is. "I'm over here at your could be babymama's house." I heard Eugene asking her what the fuck she was talking about. She then explained to him what was up. The phone hung up and about 15 minutes later there was a knock on the door. I went to open it and it was Eugene! He stood there with anger in his eyes. Chris and Ashley came from around the corner to see who it was. We all stood there speechless. O it was about to be some shit......

TO BE CONTINUED